# Please, Not That

a collection of short stories

Anna Umea

# Copyright and Acknowledgments

First published by Anna Umea Self Publishing, 2019



Paperback Edition © August 2019. ISBN: 978-1-9993199-2-2

My thanks to the people that gave encouragement and feedback for their support, insight and honesty.

# Preface

These stories have been created over a period of time and while diverse in their narrative and structure all share a context in the paraphilic fetish that involves wearing and using diapers (or nappies, if you're in the Commonwealth).

Some of the stories (such as the title one, 'Please, Not That') are cathartic and represent a need to share inner angst, but have also found an audience online that welcome a different perspective on the fetish or are just seeking something other than trope-ridden masturbatory material.

Other stories are whimsical or playful in nature. The whole 'Supersoft' series was written to tease web forum admin that have to deal with spam posts on a daily basis and other stories intentionally seek to mislead the reader.

Sometimes I also stray into the tropes of the erotica genre. After writing 'Decadent' it was fun to subvert expectations by abandoning my normal style in 'Decadent Deux'.

The final two entries relate to a fictional world setting known as the Diaper Dimension. Although initially created to allow a satirical (and beautifully written) story that sought to include (and gently teased) as many of the genre's fiction tropes as possible the author kindly provided permission for others to set their stories in this world.

The initial story in that setting, Alisa's Adventures in the Diaper Dimension included use of a portal to travel between our world and the diaper dimension, with stories building on controlled use of that portal and/or exploring the natively born inhabitants of the dimension.

Characterized by a physical size and power imbalance between human adults (known as Littles) and a giant race with superior intellect and technology (the Amazons) a number of well written books and stories have emerged that explored those power imbalances and used them to progress a range of plots covering multiple fictional genres.

It was this exploration of power dynamics and emotions that showed me fetish fiction can be about more than the fetish, inspiring my own writing.

Why short stories? They're much easier to finish, most of my inspiration comes in the form of a single concept or twist, and (as with my first story, 'Taming Your Amazon') they allow very different structures and approaches to sharing fiction.

I write for my own benefit, emotional release joined by pride and enjoyment at the works. This book exists because of that pride and enjoyment: I want others to share and enjoy the stories too.

# Stories List

# Decadent

Pizza delivery is the peak of Western decadence. Not only is someone making a meal for you, not only are they delivering it to your door, not only are they charging you an African's week's wages for this, but the meal they deliver is nutritiously bankrupt, a hedonistic luxury consumed purely for pleasure.

I opened the door and welcomed my decadence.

The boy that delivered it drove to my house so he had to be at least 17, even if he didn't look it. His features suggested Pakistan but his clothes were pure Birmingham, a shell suit and expensive trainers covering his slim youthful frame. We swapped money for pizza, then I looked him in the eye and gave him a night to remember.

“Could you help me? I need a change.”

Pakistani origins or not his reply was pure English middle class, with an accent to match. “Erm, sorry?” he asked, confusion giving him an attractive vulnerable look.

I reached down and slowly started to lift the hem of my skirt. It was short to start with, a simple A line style with a lace edged slip underneath. Watching his face I could tell the moment he saw the lace, his wide eyed gaze flicking in surprise and anticipation.

“My nappy needs a change,” I told him, my sultry voice drawing his eyes back to my face.

I could see him translating that into a context his brain could handle, something he struggled to achieve. He looked back down at my bare thighs, my skirt now high enough to show the stretched plastic that held them apart, slight discoloring making evident the truth of my admission.

He actually stepped back in shock, looked back up at my face. I smiled at him and asked sweetly, “Will you help?”

Next time I'm definitely setting up a camera. The range of expressions on his face would go viral, even if they did end with him visibly exerting some self control.

“I'm sorry Ma'am,” he said, “I'm at work and I have other customers' pizza in the car going cold.”

I frowned, as much at being a Ma'am not a Miss, vicious feedback that I look my age. He didn't notice, he'd already turned and walked away. As he got into his car I heard him burst out laughing, a reaction he'd so politely suppressed in front of me. Impressive for a young man, a credit to his parents – but no use to me.

Oh well. At least I had pizza.

# Faking Feces

Vivian looked at the banana. She'd eaten many in her life, some of them salaciously, a visual tease to the boys that could see her, making them shift uneasily in their seats.

She wasn't going to eat this one. She'd bought it for another reason, waited for it to ripen, made sure she was alone and could safely play.

She didn't play often, a shared house inconvenient when the games can be heard, or smelled. Her room was private enough, a lockable cabinet providing additional discretion, but she still liked the house empty when she wanted some fun.

Vivian looked at the banana. This was meant to be fun.

The internet had told her it was a great thing to do. All of the sensation, none of the smell. Immediate results, simple clean up. Countless anecdotes and variations on how to approach this new way to explore her interests. She'd decided to keep it simple: lubricate, insert, sensation, outcome. Well outcomes; the banana and what it would do to her.

Vivian looked at the banana. Now the moment of insertion was upon her she felt queasy, uncertain. Did people really do this?

She peeled the banana, looked at its naked form, the enticing aroma making her hungry. Lifting her skirt she sat on the bed, a disposable below her, clean and still fragrant. Taking the banana in one hand she reached for the bottle that would make it slippery; more than it was.

This felt wrong to her. She didn't do this to her vibrator, arousal providing an innate solution. But her vibrator went somewhere else; this banana would breach new territory. No amount of arousal would make that an easy passage.

Vivian looked at the banana. This wasn't arousing her.

She sighed, fastened the diaper snugly around her, draped her skirt modestly over the top and looked at herself in the wardrobe mirror. Maybe this worked for people on the internet but she was in her room, in her home.

Vivian looked at the banana. She lifted it to her mouth, took a bite. It tasted good, of childhood and innocence, a simple pleasure. Why insert when she could taste, gain sustenance, let nature take its course. The banana would reach her diaper soon enough.

# [SPAM warning] Supersoft Fluffies

## Announcing Supersoft Fluffies, a new adult protection product.

A new paradigm in disposable garments designed to provide necessary protection from unwanted leaks and solids, Supersoft Fluffies assure your loved one stays secure.

Scientifically constructed to prevent expansion when wet Supersoft Fluffies offer extensive comfortable padding at all times, preventing clothing from getting too tight during wear. This exquisite soft comfort has been constructed with a high waist and generous fitting at the legs to maximize the sensation of all encompassing cover.

The science doesn't stop there! Paper thin wearable electronics have been incorporated into the plastic exterior, avoiding the weight and bulk of batteries through innovative contact patches that generate the trace amounts of electricity required. The patches are carefully designed to react with urea and other unpleasant chemicals expelled by the body, converting their chemical energy into electricity. The remaining liquid is much less toxic, vastly reducing the risk of rash and improving comfort during extended wear.

A clever permeable membrane in the layers nearest the wearer's skin draws the urine away from the body and provides a constant supply to the electronics. Clean moisture is permitted back through, offering the wearer tactile feedback on the state of the garment and whether it remains dry.

The electronics do make the plastic backing on Supersoft Fluffies thicker than wearers might be used to but this gives the waterproof cover extra strength and you'll find the added functionality provided more than justifies any additional crinkling sounds: The electronic systems can interact with our patented Fluffies SuperApp, available on all modern mobile devices, and provide confirmation of whether the Supersoft Fluffies diaper has been used, whether it needs to be changed and, through artificially intelligent systems applying careful analysis of flow rate, previous usage and time of day, a prediction of when the next change is likely to be needed. The Fluffies SuperApp can even track usage and pre-order new supplies so that you never run out!

As many of the adults for whom Supersoft Fluffies are bought are vulnerable or in situations precluding direct access to their nether regions the Supersoft Fluffies are fastened with patent pending Eletabs(R). While looking like normal disposable diaper tabs these record the fingerprint of the person fitting the Supersoft Fluffies diaper and will only open when the same fingerprint is matched to the person trying to undo each of the Eletabs(R).

As the fingerprint matching is performed by the built in electronics it is impossible to remove the garment while dry, helping avoid any Supersoft Fluffies being wasted. So that this wont inhibit important scheduled activities such as bath time or a pre-bed change Supersoft Fluffies include a medicinal coating that induces temporary incontinence, guaranteeing swift use of the garment. This impermanent effect lasts only a few hours, with most of our happy customers regaining full control within a couple of days.

Customer feedback during testing revealed that an override for the fingerprint detection was highly desirable to support scenarios involving multiple carers (shift patterns, illness, etc) so it is possible to use the

Fluffies SuperApp to override the initial fingerprint by capturing a new one on the mobile device. This is transmitted and programmed into the garment's electronics, allowing new carer to open the Eletabs(R) to change the Supersoft Fluffies diaper. As this may otherwise negate the security offered by Eletabs(R) the addition of this feature has required additional electronic checks which mean that a non-invasive DNA comparison between the finger used to open the diaper and the person wearing it is made before the Eletabs(R) will open, with a match keeping the Supersoft Fluffies diaper firmly fastened.

Order now at all major adult medical suppliers (and a few minor ones) or read our customer testimonials to find out how they feel about Supersoft Fluffies.

*Customer Testimonials*

David from Ohio writes, “I bought a sample pack of Supersoft Fluffies for my wife Selena to help her with an occasional bed wetting problem. They were an instant success with not a single wet mattress since. Selena does now complain at times that she's permanently in diapers but I think it's a worthwhile exchange for that night time security.”

Fatima got in touch with us from Arizona, “I bought Supersoft Fluffies for my own use and didn't know I couldn't undo them myself. The first one I tried was totally saturated before I gave up and waddled out of my room to ask my housemate to help. She laughed but found the override easy to use. I had to promise to let her put me in a new one before she'd change me and I'm now on my third pack. Is there any way to override them myself?”

Supersoft Fluffies are even popular internationally. Hannah from Germany shared her experiences, “Hilfe, wie kann ich die Inkontinenz aufhalten? Mein Freund sagt, er habe es satt, meine Windel zu wechseln und es ist sehr teuer, neue zu kaufen”

But we think Charlene from Florida says it best, “Oh thank you thank you thank you for Supersoft Fluffies <3<3<3<3<3<3<3”

So order yours online today at http://SupersoftFluffiesForLife.com or Like us on InstaTwitFace for a free sample pack.

# Please, Not That.

*A short story of strong emotions.*

"Cabbage!" I think, that's what I fancy. Turning smartly on my heel I head back towards the front of the shop. Cucumbers, courgettes, cauliflower, strawberries.. wait? Strawberries? In the veg aisle?

Eventually I spot the cabbages, reject the wrinkly Savoy options, decline the red cabbage (although if I'd been cooking, maybe) and opt instead for a crisp fresh white cabbage. It's an odd choice for dinner but I've learned to listen when my body made demands.

Of course, cabbage does not a meal in itself make. “Perhaps some cheese would go well,” I decide, so I saunter past the milk and the butter, reluctantly past the trifles and cheesecakes and find the cheese. Ah, a nice strong mature cheddar, that should do the trick.

As I reach towards it I realize I'm almost stood in a puddle. My open toe sandals, ideal for the sunny weather, would give me scant protection against that wetness. I carefully lean over and claim a pound of creamy goodness, then escape down the aisle towards the delicatessen counter. This store is usually so good at keeping the floor clean, spillages coned off and cleaned up in no time. Perhaps I should let a member of staff know, this must be a recent issue.

It doesn't take long to secure a few slices of pastrami, to add some texture and a different flavor to the cabbage and cheese, and I ponder whether anything else is needed. I fear the choices so far were going to lead to just too dry a meal, so.. ah, yes! Dinner would be finished nicely with some mayonnaise. I know I could make this from scratch but I'm also partial to a particular commercial brand, which I set about hunting down.

The aisle with the oils and sauces in it didn't have any mayo. It did have a man in it, gray hair, that I nearly trip over, only just seeing him in time. I concede to myself that I maybe wasn't paying full attention, searching for the mayo, but convince myself nonetheless that it was really his fault, crouching down as he is. It was only his bright red t-shirt that saved him, catching my eye at the last moment.

With surprise I realize that the man is crouching over another puddle. He avoids eye contact and leans to look under the shelves. Skirting carefully around him I try to explain this strange behavior. Aha, the fridges with the cheese are on the other side of the shelving, and he must be Maintenance trying to track down which one was leaking. I smile to myself, I'm in no danger of leaking today.

The next corner reveals Mayo, in light and full evil fat forms, with the larger container on an unexpected sale that makes it the cheapest option. I put a tub into my shopping basket and move through the store to find some ice cream before heading home.

Sat watching a documentary on TV, I take a slice of raw cabbage, dip it into the large pool of mayonnaise on my plate and lift it to my mouth. A delightful crisp snap as I bite into it releases the flavor of the cabbage, mingling with the smooth mayo and leaving me wondering why I don't do this more often. Between the cabbage, the cheese and the mayo I barely even touch the pastrami, starting to work through the plate full of food.

It doesn't take long before my stomach starts to grumble. I've always found cheese filling but I'm caught by surprise at how quickly the cabbage was satisfying my appetite. Tasty as it is though, I don't want to stop, and quaff most of my glass of water to wash down the food I've already eaten. Foolishly at this point I tuck straight back in, and clears my plate.

“That was good,” I tell myself, intentionally ignoring that I've just eaten half a cabbage and far too much cheese. I know there's ice cream waiting, if I pretend I'm not too full. Perhaps a few minutes to let the main course settle wont hurt. After those few minutes I pause the documentary and seek out the ice cream. Salted caramel, rich, creamier than the cheese and so good. I greedily finish the whole pot.

With another glass of water I lean back and enjoy the documentary. It's an old one, a mix of black and white footage and a silky voice-over from a famous British actor, since deceased. Aware of my full stomach I relax, my patio door open to allow a gentle breeze, the cats playing in the garden.

Twenty, perhaps thirty minutes later, I shift slightly in my seat. With nobody else at home there would be no harm in relieving some internal pressure and without conscious thought, I gently squeeze out some air.

It isn't air.

Freezing rigidly in disbelief I try to convince myself that I had merely broken wind, and that the horrid sensation I'd just felt was not.. but I knew. There could be no lying about this. Furiously I thought whether my body had warned me, but it had not, and now it was too late. Pausing the TV I gingerly stand, walk upstairs and strip off my now contaminated clothing.

My skirt goes into the wash pile. The black denim will survive well enough, without a stain. My underwear comes into the shower with me; it needs rinsing clean more than I do. Fortunately it's everyday wear, no expensive lace to be ruined.

This isn't the first occasion. It's been many months though, maybe a year. Sure, some foods cause problems and I really should see about a diagnosis of IBS but I do normally at least get 40 seconds warning, all that's needed to avoid humiliation. Even with just the cats around, it's humiliating.

Still, I know I can manage this situation. Indeed, what's about to happen is entirely overkill, but I'm annoyed and scared it'll happen again. I retrieve something entirely misnamed a brief, because briefs don't fasten at the waist with sticky tape, aren't covered in a soft pliable plastic, and the ones I normally wear are nowhere near half an inch thick.

This one is.

Putting it on takes just a few moments. All that practice had to count for something. Yet this time it feels different, there's no thrill, no sense of naughtiness, it just leaves me pensive. Wearing these things for fun and fantasy is one thing; wearing one because of genuine need is new, concerning, somehow weirdly feels like an adult act – perhaps because I'm the one being responsible about this, rather than the wish fulfillment of having it done to me.

A clean skirt, a coordinated top and I'm done. I wear the same bra, it wasn't a matching set anyway and why create more laundry. Strange justification, given the clean top, which itself makes no sense: I'm not going out again today, even if I hadn't had to change my underwear. Maybe I just want something about my attire to look right. Perhaps this isn't the time for logic.

The evening passes slowly. Every internal signal from my body gets scrutinized, and I can't concentrate on television, reading, anything. The cats come and go, they're not bothered.

I am.

My new padded underwear stops feeling so new. I know it'll be a while before it nears capacity, and while it's holding just liquids I can pretend this is just another playtime. Unscheduled, I'd intended to be all grown up this week – hence being safe from leaks in the supermarket. So much for that plan. But these things cost money so I take the opportunity to at least get something from the situation.

My ideal outcome is a quiet night, a clear signal from my body when it's ready, a chance to reclaim my adulthood. Fate has other plans. This time I don't assume it's air, almost leap from my seat and dash for salvation. It's not enough, and for the second time in the evening I'm shamed.

I should be mortified. Part of me understands this, wants to embrace it, burst into tears and give up. Instead I almost celebrate: My skirt and other clothing is still clean, and quickly removed. The so-called briefs that protected it come off next, and yet again I find myself in a shower to get clean. The act of showering is efficient but mechanical, I'm doing it because it needs to be done.

It's later, in bed, further protection in place, that the flurry of thoughts hits me, that I relent and let the emotions come. I don't enjoy being in tears but sometimes it's the right response. Incontinence is a frequent fantasy, but stays safely in that realm. Permanent protection can be discreet and is manageable, but there's an impact on activities, social interactions and confidence. I like the idea of having no control but know I'd hate the reality.

But the fantasy is never double incontinence. The age play doesn't go there either; the smell and mess is too unpleasant, too much to handle. I feel doubly betrayed. I don't want to have no control, and if I had to, that's not the control I'd want to lose. This isn't fun, this is purgatory.

Am I doomed to needing constant cover? Absorbency maybe isn't so necessary, something thinner might work. But that's not the issue, the clean garment is irrelevant. It's what happens if it stops being clean. I can't hide that, my friends and colleagues would notice immediately. I'd notice immediately and that's bad enough. My brain racing, I try to think how to manage this issue. Maybe surgery? The classic cork gag? Work from home and abandon my social life? Preemptive cleansing? Or just stop eating when I'm not going to spend the next few hours at home. That means eating in the evenings and going to bed in uncertainty.

Like I am now.

Will I wake up soiled? Not a question I want to ask every night, and it's frightening me enough to defer sleep tonight. Surely I'll be fine? This must be a one-off, there must have been a strange pesticide on the cabbage, possibly too much mayonnaise, or it was discounted because it was going off. I've cleared my system, haven't I? It can't happen again, it wont keep going on tomorrow, the day after, next week? The rest of my life?

A cat jumps up, snuggles close, falls asleep. I join her. Tomorrow.. I'll find out.

# The Aftermath

Being raped isn't meant to be fun. Sure, I had the same rape fantasies so many women enjoy, that yearning for a strong relentless man to take me against my will, the imagined degradation more arousing than the act itself. But those fantasies should always stay that way; nobody pretends the reality would be like that.

It wasn't.

In a way I was lucky. Being raped could easily have destroyed my self confidence, left me fearful of men, a perpetual victim at a psychological level. Instead, in a surprisingly superior alternative, I was gang raped.

I'd still have taken the “Not tonight, thanks” option, had it been available. If I had been given a choice.

Instead they overpowered me. If I'd been raped I would have felt guilt at not resisting enough, wishing I'd struggled more. You can't struggle with a man on each arm, another two tugging at an ankle each, others watching and laughing. I could have shouted but there was nobody to hear, nobody that could come and help, so I saved my energy. They didn't like that, they wanted me to scream. I didn't care what they wanted; they were getting more than they deserved anyway.

Don't ask me to describe the physical experience. Sure, they were kind enough to use sunflower oil. They weren't kind enough to not need it. I started off in denial, trying to pretend it wasn't happening. It was happening, and that left me in horror, gasping as I tugged futilely with my held limbs. But by the time the third had dropped his trousers I'd come to terms with it, and that's where the blessing of having so many of them revealed itself.

I got bored. Somehow my brain dissociated itself from the vicious misuse of my body and instead I ended up analyzing the situation, looking closely at the men. It helped, later, when I described them to the police, picked them out of identity parades. It didn't help at the time, when I actually laughed at one that couldn't perform. He didn't rape me, just kicked my leg. That hurt, but it'll heal.

The final man was the one that really hurt me. “I don't want no sloppy seconds,” he declared. Too right, although rather more than seconds. I could almost empathize with him on that. But not on how he chose to avoid it: He asked his friends to flip me over, and I lost a different virginity.

Even that wasn't degrading. By then I just wanted it all over with, one way or another. But this last man didn't use the lubricant, impromptu though it was. He used rough force, enough that it must have hurt him too, left me surprised he could continue after that initial pain.

He's the one that did the damage. The others hurt me too; the police report included words like abrasions, bleeding, inflammation and some that were new to me like haematoma and hymenal cleft. Those would mostly heal, no long term damage. Not physical damage anyway.

That was the other part of the police report. More words like bruising and swelling, but also 'fissures' and the three that mattered: pudendal nerve damage.

The doctors tell me that those are the primary cause of my new incontinence. No, I don't wet myself. The other sort.

They've promised treatment. Electrical stimulation, but they sounded skeptical even as they described it. Physiotherapy, possible medications, potentially even surgery. But none of that was possible until the other damage healed. The fissures are the key issue, even with care they're going to take over a month, maybe two.

I can handle that. I might even be out of diapers by the time of the trial. If my lawyer lets me – she wants me to look like a victim. I might not have a choice; the doctors didn't sound hopeful, even when they were trying to convince me.

It's strange, rape fantasies never leave you in diapers. Let alone for life.

# [Not SPAM] Supersoft Sleepwells

Announcing Supersoft Sleepwells, a unique and innovative approach to night time care and protection.

Following the tremendous reception to the magnificent Supersoft Fluffies the research scientists at http://SupersoftFluffiesForLife.com have been working hard to invent a new paradigm in comfortable protection. Supersoft Sleepwells introduce a new registered design that incorporates favorite features of Supersoft Fluffies then boosts functional excellence further through new and exciting options for carers and wearers alike.

In response to strong demand for overnight protection guaranteed not to leak Supersoft Sleepwells discard legacy diaper design and focus on extensive absorbency and elimination of traditional egress points. That's right, the new Supersoft Sleepwells dispense entirely with openings at the top of the legs, instead extending right down to cover the legs and feet. Naturally an overnight garment will be worn lying down so the waistband represented a further risk vector and has also been removed. Instead Supersoft Sleepwells enfold the wearer right up to the neck, fastening across the shoulders with the same patent pending Eletabs(R) that have proven so popular on Supersoft Fluffies.

While competing products have opted for a waterproof sleeping bag style design the Supersoft Sleepwells exhibit the attention to comfort and practicality our customers demand through inclusion of sophisticated components that address potential challenges. To retain that leak proof shoulder fastening Supersoft Sleepwells feature integrated sleeves into which the wearer's arms can be inserted. These allow a range of movement on the inside to prevent cramping but are carefully constructed to keep hands safely away from the shoulder openings or genital areas.

In addition to this early research swiftly discovered that wearers were struggling to sleep in the absence of a thick diaper between their legs, requiring the physical feedback of secure and thirsty absorbent material to reassure them that they were safe and secure overnight. Supersoft Sleepwells thus provide that feedback through extensive absorbent padding between the thighs, offering several inches of width and depth that provide a constant reminder to the wearer of their secure protection.

That security is further assured by the Eletabs(R) fingerprint and DNA matching that validates that it is a carer providing a change. Powered by the same chemical transformations as Supersoft Fluffies the Supersoft Sleepwells share the medicinal coating that promises a ready supply of liquid fuel through temporary incontinence. Harnessing the greater internal surface area of Supersoft Sleepwells that medicinal coating has been supplemented with a new muscle relaxant that encourages restful sleep. Although carefully controlled to wear off overnight to allow a bright and active daytime the muscle relaxant has been observed to impact on rear sphincter muscles but our carers tell us it's great to assure solids are eliminated overnight as this gives them an easier job during the day.

Obviously in a recumbent position gravity itself works to prevent straightforward release of the bladder, risking discomforting retention of unwanted liquids. To support the Eletabs(R) we've built in a new and expanded suite of paper thin electronics that not only power the fingerprint and DNA sensors but can now also actuate micro-motors carefully embedded at the front and rear of Supersoft Sleepwells. These micro-motors provide a vibrating sensation below the rib cage and from the kidneys down the posterior that simulates the rubbing a medical professional would use to express the bladder and encourage release of the bowels. In addition to the medical benefits of delivering painless and assured elimination of all waste products this approach provides a pleasurable massage to the wearer, boosting their satisfaction and aiding swift sleep.

Demonstrating a commitment to care and risk reduction the embedded electronics also include vital monitoring with automated notification to the carer and medical authorities should the wearer require assistance.

Although thoroughly covered in a choice of decorative and waterproof NoTears[tm] rip-proof plastic some carers expressed concern that a wriggling wearer may damage their Supersoft Sleepwells or (if circumstances prevent use of bed rails) themselves so at the top of each arm and at the toes there are strong loops that can be safely fastened to the bed or any standard hospital restraint system. Although this will prevent the wearer from getting up to go to the toilet that's not going to be a problem when they're wearing Supersoft Sleepwells.

In fact, not only are these our warmest ever diaper, all Supersoft Sleepwells come with a 'Return and replace' warranty that they will not leak within the first three days of continuous wear.

Order now at all major adult medical suppliers (and a few minor ones) or read our customer testimonials to find out how they feel about Supersoft Sleepwells.

*Customer Testimonials*

Our very first testimonial came from Fatima in Arizona, who writes, “My roommate signed me up to help test your new Supersoft Sleepwells and now demands that I go to bed in one every night. She's told me I can go back to Supersoft Fluffies if I can go a whole night without messing but that hasn't happened yet. Why are you doing this to me?"

Trent in Wisconsin wrote to tell us, "I didn't believe your three day warranty so my wife Julie hasn't been changed now for 83 hours. She keeps begging for a clean diaper but there hasn't been even a suggestion of a leak. These things are amazing!"

More praise from Lilian who wrote to us all the way from England, which is in England. She tells us, "My girlfriend Kelly had problems sleeping so I suggested Supersoft Sleepwells and she agreed to give them a try. It's fun watching her try and walk with all that padding between her legs before the muscle relaxant kicks in and she collapses helplessly onto the bed. Cleaning her in the morning is yucky but it's worth it for how that built in massager keeps her on the edge all night. I might have to try these myself!"

Validation of our health monitoring came from Frank in Texas. He let us know that, "I managed to get into it but found my arms were trapped and I couldn't get back out. Two days later I was going delirious from dehydration when paramedics broke into my house and told me they'd had an automated emergency call. I'm OK now, or will be when they stop putting me in Supersoft Sleepwells and release me from this secure hospital. Can you tell them it was all just an accident?"

But we think Kirsten from Florida says it best, recognizing the warmth and comfort promised with every Supersoft Sleepwells, "Ohhh mi godd this si soo hawt like i just cant!!!!111"

So order yours online today at http://SupersoftFluffiesForLife.com or Like us on InstaTwitFace for a free sample pack.

# The Terrible Tied Tickling Torment

"No! Stop! Please... argh!"

Natasha convulsed helplessly, grasping for his wrists, wriggling to avoid his probing fingers. It didn't help her, his greater strength pinning her down and he remorselessly tickled her just above her hips. Flailing uncontrollably Natasha felt pain as her forearm made contact, realized she'd caught him, heard a horrible wet grinding sound.

He screamed, a terrible sound, and fell back, freeing her. His hands went to his face, and already she could see blood passing through his fingers.

“Oh my god!” she exclaimed, “I'm so sorry. Are you OK?”

Ice and cloths to mop up the blood brought his bleeding under control. He looked at her, obviously in pain, his proud nose now pointing sideways, and Natasha's heart sank.

“Come on,” she said, “Lets get you to the hospital.”

The triage nurse rapidly assessed him. “We'll be with you soon,” she assured, “please wait here.”

Natasha went to find them both drinks, brought back coffee, found him sat there wincing, blinking up at her and shaking his head as she arrived. “I'm so sorry,” she said again, “but you'll be OK.”

“You're sorry?” asked a voice, “You didn't..?”

Natasha turned, found a smartly dressed woman stood there, a name tag identifying her as a doctor. “I didn't mean to,” explained Natasha, “He was tickling me and..”

“Well, lets get him sorted,” said the doctor. “Could you wait here and we'll be back soon.”

That was the last Natasha saw of him until the trial.

“He was just tickling you?” asked the prosecutor.

“Yes,” replied Natasha, not offering further detail.

“And you've been together how long?”

“A few months.” Natasha knew it was five months, two weeks and three days but her legal defense team had told her to provide only short terse answers.

The prosecutor seemed satisfied anyway, but continued with his questioning “Are intimacy and displays of affection part of your relationship?”

“Oh, yes,” said Natasha in surprise, “he's really very sweet.”

“So why,” demanded the prosecutor, “did you assault him?”

The judge hadn't been sympathetic. “Domestic violence has no excuses,” he stated, “and so I have choice but to impose a custodial sentence.”

The judicial system demanded punishments appropriate to the crime. Natasha pleaded with the judge, “Please, don't break my nose. I'll behave, agree to your sentence, but please, show mercy.”

The judge knew she would make this plea; he'd discussed it with the prosecutor and her defense team. The prosecutor had suggested an alternative but still suitable option.

“For the next four weeks,” he told her, “You will be taken from your cell twice a day and subjected to half an hour of tickling.”

Natasha gasped, but said nothing. Better than a broken nose, awful but tolerable. Just four weeks and she'd be free again, able to resume her life. At least she'd get respite on Sundays.

“She what?” asked the Governor in astonishment, “She actually struck you?”

“Yes,” replied the guard, “It was her first tickling session. We followed standard procedure, let her lie on the padded workbench, and then I went to work.”

“So Natasha,” asked the Governor directly looking at her, “Why did you assault my member of staff?”

“I didn't mean to,” sniffled Natasha, sank low in her seat, a submissive posture even without the shackles restricting her movement. “It's.. when I'm tickled.. I can't help it.”

“You're saying that you have no control?” asked the Governor, “That does not excuse assault, and you should have asked us for help with this.”

His verdict made Natasha's heart sink. Another four weeks, and he assured her that the punishment regime would be continued. But that wasn't the worse part.

“You must promise not to attack my staff,” he demanded.

“I promise. Oh, I don't want this to continue,” sobbed Natasha, “But.. When I'm tickled. I can't help it.”

“Are you saying you can't control yourself?” asked the Governor.

“Umm. Yes. Help?” begged Natasha.

“We can't forego the tickling,” said the Governor. “We can however restrain you for your own protection, if that's what you want?”

Natasha blushed as she realized the Governor expected her to ask to be restrained. “I, erm. Oh.” She paused, looked around the room, desperate to escape the situation.

The Governor waited patiently, impassive. He knew he couldn't force her into restraints, his options limited to punishment should she further misbehave.

Natasha knew she would have to do it. “Umm. Can you please restrain me when I'm tickled?” she asked, and immediately burst into tears.

The cuffs were strangely comfortable. The ones around Natasha's ankles were tethered to the bench with long ropes, allowing her to wriggle and move her legs; just not kick out at someone stood by her waist. Her wrists were fastened above her head, again on tethers that let her bring her hands to her own face, rub away the tears that had formed as they fastened her down.

The cuffs and tethers were strong too. She tested them fully when the tickling started, her fight or flight instincts demanding action, refusing to let her just lie there, accept the torment.

Her struggles were futile. The tickling continued, gentle but relentless, the guard trying to avoid hurting her but make her laugh. The laughing hurt.

Halfway through the session the guard jumped back. "Oh, you dirty," she shouted, before regaining control and stopping. She glared at Natasha and gestured to a damp patch on her uniform. "You pissed on me! Oh, that's not good."

The Governor agreed. "You promised not to assault my staff," he said, "and attacking them with urine is a revolting assault."

"I didn't meant to! I couldn't help it! I must have lost control." Natasha wept as she admitted wetting herself, horrified as much by that as the inevitable consequences it had for her.

"I've heard this before," observed the Governor, "and you know the response."

Another four weeks. She'd been there less than a day and already Natasha had managed to triple her term.

"But I can't help it," she whined, "you have to understand."

“Oh, I understand,” said the Governor, “But fitting the punishment to the crime here would be unsanitary. I can't ask the guards to urinate on you.”

Natasha was shocked into silence. She'd imagined more tickling, and suddenly realized she might be facing something much worse.

“I can however impose a punishment that's suitable to the offense,” said the Governor, “You claim you can't help wet on people? Well you can wet yourself.”

Natasha pulled futilely at her bonds. Three weeks in and she still couldn't stand the tickling, couldn't stop struggling, still needed those soft restraints that kept her safe, stopped her extending her sentence.

“Oh dear, did someone just wet herself?” taunted the guard, pausing the tickling to pat the padding over Natasha's pubic mound.

Natasha moaned, realizing that she'd lost control another way, again. She knew she'd have wet herself eventually, the 24 hour regime of wearing diapers excused only for bowel movements, and even those occasionally catching her unawares.

The tickling resumed and Natasha started laughing, forced to exhibit amusement at her suffering.

Even that wasn't what concerned her. After hearing about the outcome of the first session the judge had added an additional rider to her sentence: Natasha would have to endure her final tickling with no restraints, and demonstrate that she had the control needed to be safe for release. If she failed, the sentence would be renewed.

Natasha knew she was in trouble. In nine weeks and every four weeks after that, she faced being sentenced to another four weeks of tickling, knowing she would be diapered, forced to beg for restraints to hold her in place as she was subject to the humiliation of wetting herself, again and again.

# [Eat SPAM] Supersoft Lifestyles

Announcing Supersoft Lifestyles, the protection that gives you the lifestyle you deserve.

The choice is no longer whether to have comfort, discretion or protection: Enjoy all three by wearing Supersoft Lifestyles, truly putting control back into your hands.

Giving you access to technologies never before seen in adult comfort Supersoft Lifestyles don't compromise on the advanced features customers demand from Supersoft, incorporating new versions of Supersoft's proven wearable electronics and introducing advanced materials so unique that Supersoft Engineers created a whole new branch of Materials Science to invent them.

Using Supersoft Lifestyles couldn't be simpler, just pull on instead of your normal underwear and pull back down when your body tells you it's toilet time. No barriers, no complications, just you in full control over when and where you go. Designed for Discretion(R) your new Supersoft Lifestyles will be so thin you'll forget you're wearing them, yet they'll stay comfortably in place providing that secure protection Supersoft customers know and love.

That protection starts with our new soft cloth covering: Impermeablon[TM], a natural fiber material developed to allow the skin beneath to breathe naturally yet prevent all moisture from passing will stretch with you yet looks like normal cotton, cut in a modern sporting brief design. Nobody will be able to detect the extremely thin layer of highly hygroscopic padding that lines the inside but you'll know it's there, giving you confidence that any inadvertent leaks will be quickly and efficiently absorbed. Delivering on the ethos of giving you control the padding is not restricted to the crotch area, letting you enjoy active lifestyles other products couldn't handle.

The wearable electronics remain dormant until powered, using the same chemical energy conversions so effective in Supersoft Fluffies. Once enacted they respond to the presence of body fluids by alerting the wearer, giving you direct feedback that will help you exert control and also find a toilet in time. These alerts are through our Fluffies SuperApp on your phone but we've also incorporated the vibrating feedback that's been so popular in our Supersoft Sleepwells line. A small modification to assure you have control means that by default these vibrations will not induce further bladder or bowel release, although in deference to customer choice we have enabled an override in the Fluffies SuperApp.

It's unlikely that this will ever be required as in addition to the feedback Supersoft Lifestyles will respond to body fluids by discharging across the crotch area a swift release topical muscle relaxant that assures your visit to the toilet will be worthwhile, fully emptying your bladder. The built-in electronics work with sensors to calculate the size of the wearer and dispense a carefully computed volume of relaxant to guarantee release exactly 300 seconds (five minutes) after the initial feedback is provided. Our testers have expressed delight in the unexpected side-effect of temporarily relaxing the bowel, telling us this offers positive reinforcement that makes each trip to the toilet feel truly worthwhile, never needing to sit there wondering why they bothered.

Of course, sometimes a tiny leak becomes a bit larger. This is where Supersoft Lifestyles combine protection with discretion and afford you total confidence that wherever you are, you'll retain your dignity. Natural stretch at the waistband and leg openings mean no uncomfortable elastic will pinch or irritate the wearer, making Supersoft Lifestyles more comfortable than most underwear but means an internal reconfiguration is required should the padding reach its absorbency levels.

This is managed through both traditional means and an innovative capability possible only with Impermeablon[TM]. The padding will expand on contact with moisture, giving Supersoft Lifestyles remarkable capacity that belies their ultra slim design. Although this can result in a gentle bulge below tight clothing you will agree that this is preferable to wet clothes and an obvious puddle!

Even that capacity can of course be overwhelmed. On determining that volume has exceeding safe minimums encoded electrical impulses will be sent to the waist and leg openings, causing them to close down to a watertight fit with the wearer's skin. Only Impermeablon[TM] can achieve this fluid holding closeness without fusing to the skin or causing unwanted discomfort or damage. This closure is also triggered immediately on detection of any fecal matter, assuring retention of absolute discretion even in demanding (and smelly) circumstances.

As the closure will prevent normal removal of the garment the electronics will enable hidden Eletabs(R) that allow the Supersoft Lifestyles to be unfastened at the front and removed, just as Supersoft Fluffies. Indeed, we've ported the same Eletabs(R) technology, giving you all of the protection and features that provides including carer support and DNA validation.

Supersoft Lifestyles give you back your own life and let you lead a lifestyle that you control!

Order now at all major adult medical suppliers (and a few minor ones) or read our customer testimonials to find out how they feel about Supersoft Lifestyles.

*Customer Testimonials*

An early eager customer is Grant from Hawaii who told us, "The excitement of skydiving sometimes causes me a little loss of control so I wore Supersoft Lifestyles for my last jump. I'd tested them on ground and they're so discreet they were ideal under my jumpsuit! Unfortunately as I left the aircraft I received that telltale vibration and in panic pulled my parachute cord far too early. By the time I landed I was thoroughly empty inside, although I must say I had no leaks and falling onto my bottom didn't hurt at all with the now enhanced padding."

We were delighted to hear from Fatima in Arizona who revealed, "I convinced my room mate I needed to be allowed to try and regain control so she relented and bought me some Supersoft Lifestyles. After I pulled them on she checked that they'd synced with her phone, but I assured her it wouldn't be needed. Coming straight out of Supersoft Fluffies I still wasn't free of their chemicals so it didn't take long before her phone beeped to let us know I'd had a tiny accident. I ran straight for the bathroom but these strange vibrations kicked in, just like the Supersoft Sleepwells I have to wear at night, and by the time I reached it I was waddling and could no longer remove the Supersoft Lifestyles. My roommate insisted I go back into Supersoft Fluffies but has promised me I can try the Supersoft Lifestyles once a week"

Surprising feedback came from the Mu Omega Mu Sorority in Kansas, who have been impressively innovative. "We worked a deal with our partner Frat to give their pledges a test. Pull on a Supersoft Lifestyles, and take it off again four hours later. Easy, right? Of course, if one of our Sisters takes a liking to one of them a quick syringe of her urine squirted inside means he'll have five minutes to work out whether to fail the task or REALLY fail the task. You don't want to know what we then make them do to earn a change – and of course, with no clean underwear for them and a proven need for protection, they all accept our generous offer to safely fasten them into Supersoft Fluffies to get them home safe;)"

(We've since made a job offer to three members of the Mu Omega Mu Sorority, and look forward to them joining us after graduation.)

However, we think Alison from Florida said it best of all, "OMIGOD! I asked you for these and you've done them! Thank you! Oh, thank you!"

So order yours online today at http://SupersoftFluffiesForLife.com or Like us on InstaTwitFace for a free sample pack.

# I'm Wet.

I was wet, as she came through the door.

I wasn't wearing a diaper; I was just wet. She saw, and smiled.

I hadn't wet myself; I was just wet. As she smiled, I blushed.

I was wet, and as I blushed, she spoke.

“You're wet,” she teased.

I sighed. “I'm wet,” I admitted. Her smile widened.

“You're a messy girl,” she said, her mocking tone playful.

I played along. After all, I was wet.

“I made a mess,” I confessed. She rolled her eyes.

“Shall I clean your mess?” she asked.

“I can do it,” I promised. She shook her head.

“That's why I'm here,” she said. I nodded my head.

“And you're wet,” she restated.

“I'm wet,” I confirmed. “I'm sorry.”

She left me sat there, wet.

Later I paid her. Sure, I'd done my own washing up, but I'd splashed water all over. After I'd changed into a dry top I'd joined her, found my kitchen pristine again, her cleaning worth the wage. We drank coffee, and I wondered when she'd be back.

I'd be wet.

# Ephemeral Enuresis

It wasn't the first time I'd spread my legs and penetrated myself for erotic purposes. Some needs kick in when you're all alone, and there's no shame in seeking the simple pleasures in life.

I had made sure I was all alone. I'd kicked out my last boyfriend months before, made sure I picked a week no friends had birthdays, turned down a couple of invitations and booked the whole week off work. This was between me and my cat, and she wasn't likely to tell anybody.

I looked closely at the plastic implement in my hands. Only a few inches long but abnormally slim, barely wider than a thick wire. Still, I reflected, it was going into a very delicate part of me and slender as it was I was still feeling nervous and tense. Unsure how long it would stay sterile now I'd removed it from its packaging I didn't dare delay further and, using a finger to find the spot, carefully started to insert it into my urethra.

I'd been looking for a way to force incontinence on myself for a few years. I had long been curious how I'd cope with incontinence, and aroused by the thought that I'd be dependent on diapers, a full loss of control. At the same time I had the sanity to know that this would not be good, and so my research had focused on how I might achieve only temporary incontinence.

Hypnosis tapes weren't even a consideration. Not because they'd be irreversible but because I couldn't believe they'd actually work. Similarly just wearing and using diapers could condition me to relax and not care, but that wasn't really any better than choosing when to go.

Medication offered possibilities but diuretics just increased the flow. They didn't cause an actual loss of control. I'd tried a few too, although mainly to handle water retention: caffeine, dandelion, guarana, green tea, wondrous blends of herbs and spices; when you feel bloated once a month you try everything. Muscle relaxants were an interesting option but sustained use felt dangerous and I wasn't sure where to get them.

Neural blockers could do the job but I didn't know an anesthetist and wouldn't trust one that could agree to use them on someone just for fun. Obviously I didn't even explore the insanity of surgery. A fantasy situation of being forced by someone to wear diapers and prevented from removing them didn't translate to real life.

Which left catheters. Explicitly designed to allow unfettered relief to the bladder, liquid leaving as quickly as it enters, exiting the body through a small tube. Except that there were multiple risks with repeated catheter use, infections and the risk of muscle damage, the potential for serious health complications or actual permanent incontinence. Not something I wanted to risk and anyway, you could direct a catheter into a drainage bag or just plug the tube.

Technically I was now violating myself with a catheter. This was a one-off, the risks worth the substantial reward it would deliver.

I'd followed the instructions, used ice to numb the area and rubbed in a recommended gel that applied benzocaine and lidocaine as topical analgesics, but I could still feel the progress of the plastic into my body, the discomfort becoming pain and reaffirming my decision not to use catheters for incontinence.

This one wouldn't do that. It was too small and lacked an opening through which the bladder could empty. Its role was instead delivery of the tiny device I'd finally found on sale, a reputable healthcare company promoting its use and selling it through their retail website.

They'd provided a syringe containing sterile water, whatever that is, which I'd attached to the end of the narrow tube. Once the bright band on the catheter reached my body, indicating it had achieved the required depth inside me, I stopped, drew in a deep breath and forced myself to think about what I was about to do.

Pressing the plunger would force the water into the catheter, inflating its internal sacs that were now inside my urethra. Those were wrapped by the device I'd bought, a bioresorbable stent, and by inflating the sacs it would be expanded, pushed wide open inside me, its construction designed to prevent subsequent closure. My urethra would be held open until the stent was absorbed by my body, allowed my muscles to regain control, prevent the flow of liquid from my bladder.

Did I really want this? The device guidance stated 4-6 weeks before absorption was sufficient for the device to collapse and allow resumed control. This was my final chance to stop, be sensible, avoid several weeks of forced and unavoidable incontinence.

All that research, the expense of the device, the planning I'd done; I wasn't going to back out now. I pressed the plunger, felt a strange sensation inside me, committed myself to a new experience.

Too late to change my mind, I lay back on my bed. Contorting myself to watch what I was doing and monitor the progress of that bright band had been uncomfortable and there was still mild pain and some discomfort from the procedure but it was mental relief I needed for the moment. I had actually done it, the device's design meant nothing short of surgery could undo it and, if it worked as advertised, I now had a stent extended beyond my internal and external urethral sphincters holding them irrevocably open. Well, for a few weeks anyway. In other words, I was now incontinent.

I shivered, shook my head, found my throat dry. I had avoided drinking anything for nearly seven hours now, so that I could be sure I'd emptied my bladder before doing this, and now it was over I was feeling thirsty. There was more to though than simple dehydration, some form of psychosomatic symptom translating my mental turmoil into corporeality.

I reached back down and pulled the plunger back out from the syringe, a built-in stopper letting me know it had returned to its original position, and that meant it had drawn the water back out from the sacs, allowing them to deflate. To test this I pulled tentatively at the catheter and it slid easily out of me, looking even slimmer now it had deployed its payload deep inside.

Using a finger I poked at myself, trying to feel the stent. The residual soreness flared back into pain, discouraged me from further exploration, but otherwise everything felt normal down there. Maybe everything was normal, if my plan had failed.

It seemed sensible to assume the plan had worked, and that I no longer had bladder control. Leaning over to my bedside table I picked up the disposable diaper I'd left there, knowing it would be the first thing I needed after completing the procedure. Fastening it should have been a familiar activity, well practiced through years of intentional use, and physically I went through my normal process. Despite that I knew this was very different, and that for the first time in my life I was putting myself in a diaper because I needed it, because I'd use it whether I wanted to or not, because I could not choose otherwise.

Safely secured in the diaper I pulled on my favorite nightie, tidied up my room and threw away the catheter and syringe. I could finally have a drink, although this late in the evening I opted to stick with water, avoid the stimulation tea or coffee would offer. Doing this so late in the day was very intentional, so that I could sleep away the exhaustion I had known the nervous tension of the situation would cause.

My light supper finished I went to bed, pulled up my nightie and checked my diaper. I hadn't felt myself use it, but didn't know whether I'd be able to tell or not. The diaper was dry but I wasn't: now that I was hydrated and had time to assimilate my new situation I was receptive to the underlying driver for this strange self-imposed disability.

“I'm incontinent,” I said out loud, speaking to myself in the darkness. I could have said those words any time, but this time they were true, and that cut through me. My hand slipped inside my diaper and, well, sometimes fingers and thoughts are all you need.

Forty minutes later it was obvious I'd messed up. As my earlier hormonal boost wore off, the discomfort returned and I found myself unable to sleep, instead just lying there fretting for no reason, worrying that I'd been destructively stupid and caused myself permanent damage. I tried to console myself, retread the decision process that had brought me there, assured myself the risks were minimal and that it was all worthwhile, but logic plays no role when insomnia forces you to face the darkest hours.

Eventually fatigue overcame the discomfort and I drifted into a disjointed slumber, multiple fractured dreams that finally gave way to deep sleep. Dawn came and went, and midway through the morning a natural awakening gave me a gentle start to the day.

Struggling with multiple initial demands from my brain I rapidly sorted my thoughts and answered the immediate questions. The clock said it was nearly 11am, yes I had really done that last night and.. Oh! My diaper was very wet.

I couldn't remember using it. The stent was working! I sat up and stretched both arms towards the ceiling, a mute celebration that ended as I allowed myself to fall back onto the bed. Was I actually incontinent? I decided to quickly shower, pull on a clean diaper and enjoy plenty to drink with my breakfast so that as the morning progressed I'd find out. Hmm. Make that brunch, and maybe the afternoon.

Pulling my nightie off I headed into the bathroom to shower and took off my diaper there. Bending to pick it up for rolling, sealing and disposal I froze and looked at it in horror. Yes, I'd wet overnight but urine isn't that color. I'd clearly bled in it too – and I was still two weeks away from my next period. Panicking I ran through the house to find my computer, then ran back to the bathroom, grabbed a towel and returned to my computer. Sat on the towel I opened my browser, clicked on the bookmark I'd visited so often before and feverishly read through the guidance notes for the stent.

They said nothing about issues after insertion so I clicked on the search bar, entered the brand name and a single simple keyword: "bleeding". The first two results didn't help but the third was a FAQ on the manufacturer's website, something I wish I'd seen before. I clicked through and read quickly, then sat back and almost collapsed with relief. The catheter caused internal irritation, light bleeding was normal for the first couple of hours, and no cause for concern. Feeling a bit happier I got up and took the unsoiled towel back to the bathroom, where I put it to its intended use drying me after a welcome shower.

Back into a new disposable I enjoyed my brunch. Fruit, a cereal bar and some juice with a large cup of coffee was my normal start to the day and I added some toasted cheese so that I wouldn't need to eat again until evening. I'd planned for a quiet day, no chores to do, just my book, some TV and the jigsaw I was putting together on the dining room table.

Half an hour after drinking my coffee I could feel my diaper was wet. It was a modern design, discreetly thin until used when it would swell to alarming proportions, almost forcing a waddle as I walked. It hadn't reached that stage but had swollen enough for me to notice, and I'd been waiting for that. I'd felt no demands from my body, at no point had I needed to relieve my bladder; it had happily just emptied itself, the diaper the only reason my couch hadn't been soiled. But my immediate concern was whether I was still bleeding so I took off my skirt, untaped the diaper and pulled the front of it down.

My diaper was wet all right but there was no blood. I hadn't damaged myself, I was just incontinent. That thought sent a shiver through me and, well, my hand was busy again.

As the day progressed my thoughts turned to the next few weeks. Work didn't alarm me, even a wet diaper wouldn't be easily detected under one of my smart dresses, or a flared skirt. Any men that noticed could be easily put off with just two words: 'Lady problems'. The women might want more detail but I had a cover story prepared, one in which my own clumsiness with a self-administered swab had caused complications. That would earn me sympathy, should it be needed, but you don't probe too deeply on such topics at work.

Outside of work I needed to be more careful. Friends and family might notice, although the same cover story would suffice. I didn't have a choice now anyway, I'd be leaking whether I wore a diaper or not. Carrying a large purse wasn't my normal style but I had one that would hold a couple of spare diapers and a small packet of wipes. Diaper rash might be a concern but I could handle that at home, and voluntary use of diapers had taught me how to reduce the chances of it happening at all.

Long before dinner I decided the diaper needed changing. This was rather strange for me, intentional use gave me control over how wet a diaper got, and when it would need to be changed. This diaper had just incrementally become wetter as the day progressed, each drink exacerbating its condition with no intended input from me. I'd have to get used to that, start to better monitor my diaper's state and learn how to avoid over saturation, prevent leaks.

Another change before bed, a thicker diaper even when dry, intended for extended overnight use. I wanted a good night's sleep after all, and I knew a full bladder wouldn't be waking me. The diaper did its job, my bed dry when I woke, an evening's drinks safely absorbed by the thirsty padding.

A week off work was a holiday even when I stayed at home. Being stuck in diapers wasn't going to stop me enjoying it, and the next two days were spent visiting the stately gardens of a nearby Hall and thoroughly enjoying a shopping trip. The diapers did their job, didn't cause me any distress, just became a part of my life. Trying on clothes was a tense affair the first time I picked out a new skirt, but by the fourth shop I was treating the diapers as I would my normal underwear, something I kept discreet but otherwise perfectly normal.

Using the toilet still happened, that once a day need. When I was out it would have seemed more frequent but that was so that I could change into a clean diaper. I used the disabled toilets, the extra space extremely helpful. At some point it was likely I'd get challenged by someone thinking I shouldn't be using those, and I'd have to decide whether to reveal my diaper or not. That decision was one I was putting off, hoping it wouldn't be needed.

It was when I got home from the shopping trip that I suffered my first leak. I knew I'd get one eventually, that they're unavoidable if you're wearing diapers, but it wasn't something I wanted or looked forward to. Extra laundry, my leather couch needing a wipe clean, the carpet needing more than a wipe. Another thing to get used to for the next few weeks. I sighed, regretting the vicious reality of a diaper dependency even as I felt a thrill at being reminded of it.

The next morning I was woken by a telephone call.

“Good morning, I'm sorry to bother you.” He identified himself as a doctor at the healthcare provider from whom I'd bought the stent. “Could you confirm some details for me?” he asked.

Yes, he was talking to the right person. Yes, I had bought the stent. Yes, I had used it.

“Ah,” he said, ominously, “I was hoping we might have caught you before you inserted it.”

This worried me. It's never good to hear something like that from a doctor. “Umm. Why? Is there a problem?” I asked nervously.

“Oh, no,” he replied, “Is it performing as expected?”

“Yes,” I said, “full incontinence. I have no control at all for the next 4-5 weeks.”

"I see. Are you finding this manageable?" he asked.

"It's something I planned for," I admitted. Hell, they sold it for this purpose, this wasn't the time to be shy. "But you said you were hoping I hadn't used the stent. What's happening? Why did you call?"

"Well, we tested the stent extensively before it went on sale," he said, "Obviously we have regulatory approval to market it and the prototypes had no problems at all."

This didn't sound good. "The prototypes?" I challenged, "What about the production ones? What do I have inside me?"

"You have one of our production devices," he confirmed, "but we've identified a manufacturing issue in the batch yours is from. Now, don't be alarmed, this..."

"Don't be alarmed?!" I shouted, cutting him off, "what sort of issue? Stop prevaricating, tell me what you've done to me!"

"We haven't done anything!" he said defensively.

"What is inside me?" I demanded.

"It's a fully functional stent. The only change from what you're expecting is that it's unlikely to take 4-6 weeks to be reabsorbed," he told me.

"What? Well how long then?" I asked, "How long will I remain like that?"

"It may be the full 4-6 weeks," he said, hesitantly, "but our models suggest that it absorption will be much quicker. Your stent is very likely only going to last 4-6 days."

Relief almost crushed me. I'd been fearing the worse, and he hadn't delivered it. “Oh thank goodness,” I said, “Why didn't you just tell me that to start? You had me panicking.”

“I'm sorry,” he said, “This is difficult for me too. I can assure you that we will give you any support you need should the device cease to operate ahead of schedule, including providing you with a replacement should that be something you desire.”

That made me pause to think. The reality of incontinence was proving very inconvenient, constant diaper changes and the leak last night was just annoying, but it was also something I'd expected and did feel I could cope with. However I'd always intended this to be temporary so would a few days be all I needed?

“I'm not sure,” I said, “if it fails early then this is something we can perhaps discuss?”

“Of course,” he reassured. He gave me a direct number, told me to ring him if I had any concerns, gave me another assurance that they would provide me with support.

I guessed they were worried about legal action. A medical device that failed substantially early could get them in all sorts of trouble. But their failure might be my release, freedom from constantly wetting myself.

For the moment that freedom was still denied to me. Even at the lower end I had at least another day of incontinence to survive. Or enjoy. I put it to good use, a long walk through a national park. It required my first outdoor diaper change, the nearest public toilet a few miles away and my diaper too sodden to risk wearing further.

There was nobody in sight but I was still nervous. I had never been naked in public, and this wasn't simple nakedness, it was a diaper change. Leaving the track I hid behind thick bushes and undid the clips on my dungarees, lowering the bib to my waist and sliding them down to reveal my diaper. Fortunately this wasn't my first standing diaper change and I quickly had a clean one on, knowing it wouldn't stay that way but grateful for the momentary comfort. Quickly dressing again I returned to the track and found myself still alone, my worried precautions unnecessary.

That night I went to bed in another thick diaper, a onesie keeping my hands at bay, the babyish attire preventing very adult behaviour. Even as that thought amused me I realised that the diapers weren't arousing me any more. They were now just a part of my life, frequently uncomfortable, sometimes annoying, but never a source of genuine happiness. At that point I made my decision: When the stent was absorbed I'd return to using the toilet, revert back to using diapers only voluntarily, when I genuinely desired.

That wasn't the next day. I didn't panic, it could still be another five weeks yet, and although I was ready to discard diapers it was always intended to be many weeks before that would be an option. In good heart I finished my jigsaw, took a photograph, went shopping for a new one.

The next morning things were different. I woke up early, severe discomfort down below. It took me a minute to get out of my onesie, undo the diaper, take a look inside. Immediately I felt sick, found myself on the edge of tears, stared at the blood soaking the diaper. It was still a week until my period was due, and I'd worn a diaper for that before, knew it didn't look like this.

Forcing myself to be calm I took a shower, fastened a new diaper on, dressed myself to go out and called the doctor.

Is the stent being absorbed?"

“I don't know,” I said, and described my morning's findings.

“OK, stop there,” he told me, “I'm going to send one of our ambulances to pick you up, and we're going to give you a full examination.”

I guess that's the advantage of buying dodgy devices from a large healthcare provider. They have facilities all over, including one near enough to me that I was there under an hour later, my diaper on display to two nurses and a female doctor. Then it was just me on display, that awkward uncomfortable pose, legs akimbo, cold metal invading me in a very personal way.

Strange scans followed, x rays and something else. A large machine, loud noises, the operator hiding behind a protective shield. I was already back in a diaper by then, the blood clearly coming from my urethra but diluted by more normal waste, something I still couldn't control. Instinctively I had tried and it caused pain, as though I was being pricked by a needle deep inside.

That was five days ago. The sharp stabbing pain has gone now, but the scar tissue remains. The manufacturing error meant the stent wasn't properly absorbed, had instead broken up inside me, solid fragments cutting into me from the inside. They've said that surgery wouldn't help, that the scar tissue means a catheter isn't an option, that it might heal by itself.

They wouldn't say how long that might take. At least I wasn't in pain any more, even the discomfort had faded. I'd fantasized for so long about being incontinent, carefully arranged to temporarily experience it, enjoyed that fleeting wish fulfillment.

I shifted uncomfortably, realized my diaper needed changing again. I wasn't enjoying it now, the terrible reality of needing diapers, repeatedly wetting them, hour after hour, day after day. They'd promised to keep me well supplied, my choice of diapers from their range for as long as I needed.

That was the problem. I didn't know how long I'd need it. They didn't either, couldn't even promise me my last remaining hope: That it would end, that I'm not now stuck in diapers permanently.

It wasn't the first time I'd spread my legs and wiped myself clean between them, replaced a soaked diaper with a fresh clean one. It certainly wasn't going to be the last..

## The Supersoft Support Team

Dear Mr and Mrs Gemmins,

I am writing to you today in accordance with 15 USC 6501 which requires me to inform you regarding an online website registration made by a child in your care.

The registration was made on 4th June 2003 and at the time the age of the registrant was provided as 22. We have sadly discovered since that at the time the account was created it was in fact in the control of somebody aged 14 and a half.

Although the account owner is now over 30, married and has a child of their own we are nonetheless obliged to inform you of this registration and provide you with key information regarding the account and the site, and seek your permission to gather, retain and use data associated with the account.

Our site is http://SupersoftFluffiesForLife.com and is a commercial website promoting our fantastically popular products Supersoft Fluffies and Supersoft Sleepwells, and providing a community to the carers and wearers of these essential garments.

Although the account holder has made no purchases their posting history indicates a clear interest and potential need for our products, although out of respect for privacy and personal circumstances we have not provided a free sample pack as no direct request has been made. We are obviously happy to provide you with such a sample pack if you feel these products may be of use to your ward.

Please accept our assurances that incontinence and the need for secure protection are common in teenagers and adults, and we regret that we were unable at the time to help you appropriately care for the child in question.

Should you have further questions or desire a free sample pack then do please get in touch. We have of course already disabled and deleted the account in question but will do our utmost to rectify any harm caused by our ignorance.

Yours sincerely,

-- Supersoft Web Admin

Dear Admin,

My thanks for your thoughtful letter to Mr & Mrs Gemmins, who passed it to me. I am the wife and mother to the child of the account holder and it has been an interesting and revealing few days. A cursory examination of your website led me to further investigate the computer and browsing habits of my husband, an educational experience that has addressed several of my concerns with our relationship.

Although you may not have realized, I have availed myself of your free sample pack and darling hubby is now just as protected as our delightful baby. Due to the remarkable Supersoft Sleepwells he's actually sleeping better than our child, although during the day he does need changing just as often.

I had expected complaints and grumbling about this treatment but as my investigations (and your email) suggested, he was long overdue such caring support. My great and many thanks to you for bringing this to our attention, and I trust you will continue to provide exemplary protection products to meet his needs through the coming years.

Yours faithfully,

-- Samantha

Dear Samantha,

It is always a happy moment to receive such heartfelt praise of our products and support for our needful customers. We are delighted that you have been able to so thoroughly address his underlying issues and find a shared happiness together.

Please accept with our blessing a lifetime discount on direct orders from our site, and although we don't offer products targeting children or young teens, once your child reaches her late teens do not hesitate to apply that discount to any purchases on her behalf.

Many thanks,

-- Supersoft Customer Support

# The Blowout

Kirsty knew all about blowouts. Anybody with small children knew. It wasn't something anybody was ever taught, you learned about them the hard way. A blowout wouldn't happen while a child was safely tucked away in a cot, secure, within easy reach of a change of clothes, a washing machine, a clean diaper. No, blowouts happened in public, when it was least convenient, the child in ignorant bliss of the horror it had just caused.

The weird thing was that friends didn't realize the problem. “Oh dear, someone needs Mommy,” they'd declare, confident that Mommy could cope, would quickly and efficiently return the gorgeous tot to full cuteness. It was the parent that had to deal with the mess, the way the explosion had shot up out of the back of the diaper, somehow leaked at the legs, ruined the tights, the diaper shirt, the pretty dress.

Experienced parents knew to take a change of clothing, as well clean diapers. The cafe, the village hall, the doctor's waiting room; they were someone else's problem, they had staff to clean them. Kirsty had raised three children and they had all been her problem, their comfort and cleanliness something she had to provide, and even if they didn't know what they'd done, she did, and she had to deal with it.

So when someone else was the parent, Kirsty reflected that she should at the minimum not be dismayed. It wasn't her problem, she wouldn't have to replace the soiled clothing, gently wipe the skin, pretend this was a normal run of the mill diaper change. Unfortunately she felt only distress, the realization that this was a full blowout, and that the Mommy hadn't even noticed.

“Ewwww,” she said, “That's smelly!”

It was a white lie. The food was somehow treated; extra bulk, less smell, same awful stickiness. In a way it helped, made filling a diaper a more private function, fewer people sniffing loudly and declaring, “Oh dear, someone needs Mommy.”

Alice turned and looked at Kirsty. “Oh dear,” she said sympathetically, “Does someone need Mommy?”

Kirsty groaned. No shit someone needed 'Mommy'. She knew better than to say that, three different punishments would come from that single retort. Instead she forced a smile to join the frown on her face, looked up at Alice and provided a carefully neutral reply, “Mommy...”

Alice did that adult thing of pausing to change expression, going for the sympathetic look in an obvious 'I'd better show sympathy' way. She turned back to her friend Julie, begged forgiveness for a moment and walked over to where Kirsty was strapped immobile in a push chair. Undoing the straps long enough to lean Kirsty forward, she flipped up the back of the short dress and immediately wrinkled her nose.

“Holy mother of..” she exclaimed, before her voice trailed off. She looked across to Julie and called out, “You would not believe this! It's a full scale blowout. We're going to have to find a bathroom.”

Kirsty knew all about blowouts. She hadn't expected to suffer one, be the subject of that humiliating call across the park, see her friend Tracey look across in horror. Tracey knew all about blowouts too, and had never even had children. Sometimes people learn about them the very hard way.

Carefully standing up Tracey started to waddle towards Kirsty. The look of sympathy on her face was genuine, and Kirsty knew she wanted to provide comfort and commiserations. She just didn't want them, was embarrassed enough already, just wanted to get clean.

“Tracey! Come back here.” demanded Julie. Tracey stopped, looked at Kirsty in consternation, clearly torn between friendship and the fear of disobedience. Friendship doesn't come with punishments though so when she turned and unsteadily made her way back to Julie, Kirsty silently shared thanks.

The world turned around her, and Kirsty could no longer see her friend. Alice had wheeled her around and was pushing her determinedly up the path. “Come on Sweetie,” she said, “Lets get you clean and beautiful again.”

Kirsty knew all about beautiful too. This wasn't something she had ever claimed, and although the occasional unguarded look on Alice's face showed genuine affection and the love of a mother, she couldn't believe a thick diaper and pigtails made her beautiful now. Sure, the portal had changed her body, the tired lines and stretch marks of a well used body in its forties gone, replaced by a beach ready body that looked – and felt – in its late teens. Her new body's lithe youthfulness was spoiled by poor muscle definition and wide, broad hips, which she'd decided were worth the chance to feel young again, but she was being treated as even younger, nearer 18 months than 18 years.

But beautiful? No. Not with the freckles she'd somehow acquired, even if they did help her face match the outfits she was forced to wear.

“Why the frown, gorgeous?” asked Alice. “You're much prettier when you smile, it really lights up your eyes. Julie says she loves your face when you smile, the dimples and freckles make you just adorable.”

Kirsty had heard this before, so many times she'd lost count. She'd lost count of many things, repeated humiliations, public embarrassments and private mortification. Her memory was good, mentally she was in surprisingly good health, adapting well to what had once been so strange a situation. She didn't seem to be aging here, her body retaining its youthful elegance, no matter how many years passed, the promise of the advertisement kept, and that promise extended to her brain, keeping her sharp and aware.

Sadly aware. The advert hadn't mentioned that her young body would not be under her control, that forced adoption by someone claiming to be her new Mommy was inevitable, that her perpetual youth would be lived in perpetual babyhood. Yes, she was aware of that.

A good memory still loses track of the prosaic, the things each day holds, the forced feedings, the mornings trapped in a playpen and the afternoon naps. Even the changing of a diaper becomes mundane, an uncomfortable embarrassment replaced by another, a temporary respite from dismal damp.

“Here we are,” gushed Alice, pointlessly telling her charge they'd reached the bathroom. Kirsty knew this building, knew the flap inside that folded down from the wall, knew she fit easily onto it and that she couldn't undo the strap that would hold her in place. She'd lost count of the diaper changes even just here, the trips to the park seldom short enough for her to stay clean throughout.

Kirsty wasn't incontinent. At least, she hadn't been. Giving birth had weakened her control but she had still had it, just the occasional emergency dash to the nearest toilet. Coming through the portal fixed even that, and for a few hours she'd reveled in the choice she had to delay those bathroom breaks, no longer hostage to the nearest facilities. It was a naive joy, replaced by a permanent delay. She couldn't remember the last time she'd used a toilet, never needed the facilities. She didn't know if she had control any more, after days, weeks and months of only using a diaper the body stops worrying about such an irrelevance.

Strapped to the padded shelf Kirsty looked up and reached out to Alice. She hated playing the cutesy toddler but it made Alice happy, and a happy Alice treated her much better.

“No Darling,” apologized Alice, “Mommy has to get you clean first. We can cuddle afterwards.”

Kirsty lowered her arms again, her simple point made, and really she was glad Alice had that priority. The park path wasn't smooth and every bump, every little jolt had transmitted through the pushchair into her diaper, reminding her its revolting contents, spreading it further. Her unwelcome, repetitious and intimate familiarity with being soiled had inured her somewhat to the situation but she still hated it, wanted it gone. She felt the diaper shirt being unfastened between her legs, her tights pulled down, then her shoes being removed and the tights taken off completely.

“Oh my,” sighed Alice, “you can't wear those again.” She pulled out a small plastic bag, normally used for dirty diapers, and put the filthy clothing in it. She unstrapped Kirsty, lifted her up and stripped the dress and onesie off her.

Kirsty stood there, wearing just a heavy diaper and pale blue ribbons, in her hair. She watched Alice examine the clothing, saw for herself the horrible state of her onesie, prayed it wouldn't be put back on her. Alice fortunately reached the same conclusion, thrust it into the same bag containing the tights.

“Even your dress is dirty, but it's just a small patch by the hem. I'll wash that down Sweetie, or you'll have to go home in just your diaper.”

Kirsty knew better than to comment on her clothing, but allowed a quiet smile to show her satisfaction with the compromise. The day was warm and, while she was permanently in diapers, and she knew that in the pushchair her dress would ride up and reveal her shame to passers-by, she still wanted it on, even the smallest concession to covering her diaper was worthwhile. But first, she wanted a clean diaper.

“What's wrong Kirsty?” begged Alice, obvious concern lining her face. Kirsty realized with horror that she'd let her true feelings show in her facial expression, right as she'd been mentally berating herself for falling into the mental trap of wanting a diaper, rather than just wanting to be taken out of this dirty one.

Kirsty recovered fast. She'd learned well, knew how important it was to keep Alice on her side, knew the buttons to push. “Sticky!” she sniffed, concentrating on not saying any more than that, and especially not asking to be changed.

Alice melted a little, reached forward and gave Kirsty a quick hug around the shoulders. “Awww, you poor thing,” she acknowledged, “Lets get you out of that horrible diaper.”

For once the pair shared a moment, full unanimity, all guile and pretense unnecessary as they looked at each other in agreement.

A swift change, Alice well practiced, soft wipes quickly leaving Kirsty's skin smooth and pristine, a light dusting of powder and clean padding, firmly fastened, securely sealing Kirsty into a gently scented leak proof prison that she knew would soon be a torment once more.

“There,” celebrated Alice, pulling Kirsty's dress back on and giving her the promised hug, “all clean and beautiful.”

Sure, thought Kirsty. Until the next time. She knew there'd be a next time, it was inevitable, unavoidable, one of the few certainties in her new life.

Yes, Kirsty knew all about blowouts.

# Taming Your Amazon

or

## How to Survive and Thrive When Little : A Pamphlet from the Little Liberation Front

*Foreword*

This publication is targeted at Littles entering or already within an asymmetric relationship with one or more Amazons. Although ending the relationship is frequently the primary goal in such a situation this is seldom achievable without substantial effort and elapsed time.

Through understanding and adopting approaches from this guidance, a Little can minimize their chances of forced regression, entering an orphanage or undergoing irreversible physical or mental deterioration.

*Chapter 1 : Understanding Your Amazon*

Congratulations! You are now the proud beneficiary of your very own Amazon who, with the right treatment, can provide you with years of entertainment, security and emotional support.

### Rule One : Your Amazon Loves You

In almost all cases it is a female Amazon that adopts a Little[1], and we will assume you have acquired a typical female. She will be genetically

---

1 Insufficient research into male Amazon motivations means full guidance is not available at this moment in time. Most of the techniques in this pamphlet work equally well on males, although some caution may be required and the commentary on breastfeeding should be disregarded.

incapable of caring for a Little without falling in love, and very likely lost all emotional control even before you became family.

This love will guide almost all of her actions, even the ones that cause (or that you feel cause) you harm. Understanding this is key to manipulating those actions and minimizing perceived or actual harm. Your safety and happiness do actually matter to her, and these are levers you can use to your own benefit; subsequent chapters explore specific scenarios in which this can occur.

Even more powerful though is that your Amazon will love you even more, and be far more amenable to your needs and desires, if she feels that love is reciprocal. This should thus always be an immediate target, with vestiges of love – fake or otherwise – demonstrated within the first few days and a close loving relationship rapidly built.

*Case Study 1-Negative*: Charlotte was captured in her mid-20s by a middle-aged Amazon couple and understandably hated her loss of autonomy and freedom. When the couple thought they were being kind by helping Lotty into diapers, pretty dresses and a comfy crib, she rebelled against them with constant screaming and physical resistance. Obviously this led to punishment diapers, hypnotic loss of continence, almost permanent pacifier use and a strained relationship with her couple. Sadly things broke down from there and after several weeks of increased detachment due to being put in daycare the Amazon couple conceded things weren't working and contacted their local orphanage. Charlotte was lost to the system.

*Case Study 1-Positive*: Aiden got picked up before even applying to university but took a pragmatic view of his new family. He did his best to adapt to the life his Amazon wanted him to lead and quickly found ways that made her happy. This in turn assured her that he was perfect for her as he was, and although Aidy had to endure several years of being babied he eventually contacted the LLF and was able to regain his freedom. Aiden is already progressing well on his toilet training and now only wears diapers at night.

As Aiden's case study demonstrates, knowing the individual drivers and goals of your Amazon can help tremendously in building rapport and surviving the early phases of a relationship. As with Littles, Amazons are very different individuals and will vary in how much time they want to spend having a cuddle, playing with their Little, pursuing their career and continuing the other elements of their life (career, social life, hobbies, etc).

## Rule Two : Be Her Baby

Almost all relationships start with at least a week of full-time care, which is a great opportunity to learn about your Amazon and find out what she likes. The common element to all relationships though is that your Amazon will have entered it because she wants a baby. Be that baby for her.

This will be challenging for you in many ways. There is the basic difficulty of acting like a baby, especially when adult impulses and responses drive you to different behavior, but more fundamental is the apparent loss of identity. You are now her baby, with the name she gives you, and your Amazon will love you more if she feels you accept this.

This doesn't change who you are. You haven't actually lost your identity, and do fiercely remember it inside. But do keep it inside, make her believe that you embrace her and the new family, and respond to your new name. Along with this, she will want you to call her Mommy. This is an area in which you can show some individuality, but only by picking your favorite from Mommy, Mama, Momma or another suitable term that indicates a mother-child relationship (or, for male Amazons, Daddy, Dada or Papa). While most Amazons (and their Littles) will prefer and be happy with Mommy many Amazons will find it endearing if you do pick a variant.

Rule Two can be particularly challenging when the Little does not share a gender with the Amazon's preference for her baby. This is frequently an issue for male Littles, with baby girls considerably more popular than the adult Little gender ratio can support. Rule Two was nearly 'Act the Baby' to emphasize and reinforce that this is just an act, but instead became 'Be Her Baby' to emphasize that your act must portray you as she wants you to be. That means treating clothing styles and colors as props for your act, and if she wants you to be a baby girl, embrace the femininity of the role[2].

It is highly likely that your Amazon is more intelligent than you, but seldom sufficiently to be a barrier. She will still act and think with emotion in addition to intellect so engage her as a well-rounded person, assume she'll pick up non-verbal cues and help her learn quickly how to best satisfy her own instincts to make you safe and happy.

## *Chapter 2 : Apparel*

Glory in your new wardrobe! Amazons love buying new clothes for their Littles and will do their best to make you the envy of their friends.

This can lead to discord, as Amazons have a distinct expectation on how a Little should be dressed.

---

2 Fighting a gender mismatch is a terrible breach of Rule Two and commonly addressed through surgical alteration to bring physical characteristics into alignment with the Amazon's preferred baby gender. However if you do actually want physical reassignment, just ask!

## Rule Three : Never Remove Apparel

You'll have to accept that frequently you're going to be put into clothing that you greatly dislike, is uncomfortable, and/or is humiliating to wear. Whether that's because you're a man being put into a lacy baby dress, or an adult woman forced into a onesie over a diaper, remember Rule Two and treat it as a prop for your act. Not to mention that sometimes it can be fun, and many Littles grow to love their pretty clothes.

Avoid indicating displeasure with the clothing you've been made to wear. Instead show positivity towards the clothing you'd prefer to wear. If you like a dress or the romper suit you've been put in, pull gently at it and express your happiness with it. Rule One will lead to you getting to wear that more often, which means less time in the clothing you don't like.

While shopping point at clothes and use a simple single word adjective to indicate your preference. Rule Two discourages lengthy descriptions of your aesthetic preferences but don't underestimate the power of 'yuck', 'pretty!' or 'nice' in helping your Amazon understand how to better make you happy.

Your clothing will become soiled through play, mealtimes and sadly leaking diapers. It is fine to express muted distress regarding this, with a simple sad 'Dirty!' and a frown showing your displeasure without being interpreted as a tantrum. Unless explicitly told to play in a dirty situation (e.g. dropped into a mud pit) do try and avoid intentionally causing soiling unless your Amazon delights in a grubby baby.

One item of apparel that you will almost immediately become very intimate with will be your pacifier. There are many designs available, both aesthetically and functionally. It's important to demonstrate to your Amazon that you can be trusted to use a 'normal' pacifier as her instant escalation will be a locking one that you can't remove yourself. These can be very uncomfortable, often filling or even stretching the mouth.

**Rule Four : Your Pacifier is Your Friend**

While building your relationship your pacifier is a great way to moderate your own voice. Many Amazons think Littles should be silent, or restricted to a very limited vocabulary, so using the pacifier to limit your speech greatly aids acceptance. You can't say things that upset your Amazon if you can't talk, but the pacifier can help in other ways too.

There's no actual difference between a quiet baby and the same baby with a pacifier in its mouth, but Amazons will instinctively assume the latter one is the better behaved. Chapter 4 will explore this further but making a good impression on other Amazons matters a lot, so setting their mental picture of you as well behaved is important. Beyond that, your own Amazon will think you delightful if you use a pacifier voluntarily, and will trust you much sooner as a result.

Don't forget the other more obvious feature of pacifiers: They exist because they make real babies more relaxed, and quiet. That will work for you too; don't be ashamed of finding comfort in a quick suck.

*Case Study 2-Negative*: Scarlett was a lithe athlete in her adult life and didn't adjust well to her new role. Because she was constrained so much to a crib, a high chair or a stroller she lost her muscle tone and developed a more babyish roundness. This delighted her Amazon but meant Letty was frequently dressed in unflattering romper suits or flat-chested dresses. Letty hated these and tried to remove them, causing multiple punishments that led to her spending more and more time restrained and unable to move freely. This vicious cycle means that Scarlett is miserable with her body shape and her clothing, and sadly now lacks the fitness to escape even with our help.

*Case Study 2-Positive*: Jayden wanted to make a good impression from the start and didn't take notice of the clothes he wore. His Amazon often put a pacifier in his mouth so Jay kept it there until she removed it herself, and consciously allowed it to help him work through stressful situations. His Amazon often told him how happy she was that he was so well behaved and started to trust him even when out of the house. This has allowed Jayden to contact our network and permanently leave that relationship, although we notice he's retained and still enjoys using his pacifier.

Some pacifiers will allow feeding or provision of medicine while worn. These are usually locking varieties and used situationally, so there is little choice but to accept them. The strategy here is to demonstrate that they're not needed through perceived good behavior during those activities normally.

You aren't the only person wearing apparel. Notice what your Amazon is wearing. Is she going to work, going on a date, dressed to play with you? Is that a new suit? Notice it, comment on it, compliment her. She'll appreciate it and you'll both feel a little happier.

## *Chapter 3 : Emissions*

Great news! You are no longer responsible for any mess (or smell) you cause. Revel in the freedom this brings.

Amazons genuinely don't think that Littles can control their own emissions. Any waste products or sickness is assumed to be beyond the conscious control of the baby (remember Rule Two) and appropriate mitigations provided. Sadly this does mean you should expect to spend most of your time in diapers.

**Rule Five : Use Your Diapers**

Here at the Little Liberation Front we have found this rule to be the most distressing for the people we're assisting, and yet it's also the one most likely to lead to at least a mild regression. Amazons worry if diapers are not constantly wet, and regularly filled, and will initially respond with food and then chemical based diuretics and laxatives. Within days though repeatedly dry diapers will inevitably lead to hypnotic or surgical adjustments that force diaper dependency, often for life.

If you ever hope to have control over your body in the future, plan ahead by choosing to abandon it now. The first few days are critical, with multiple wet diapers every day causing delight in (and providing opportunities to physical bond with) your Amazon.

*Case Study 3-Negative*: Benjamin wanted to build rapport with his Amazon and was careful to always have a wet diaper when she checked, and timed messing it for just ahead of his daily bath. He retained his bladder control by keeping his diaper dry until a check was likely then flooded it quickly in time for a change. Sadly for Bennie his Amazon caught onto the periodic nature of his wetting and messing and without him realizing fitted a wetness detector. This demonstrated his retained control, something his carer found unhealthy and undesirable, and one day Bennie was taken to his local doctor. Our subsequent physical examination following Benjamin's escape shows that he'll never regain bladder or bowel control, although he can at least now choose his own diapers.

*Case Study 3-Positive*: Evelyn kindly shared her experiences with our team even though she's declined the support and services we offer. From the outset Evie tried to relax and allow her body to wet or mess when it was ready, and has reported that this rapidly led to a loss of control. In her case her carer did not want messy diapers so she's been partially potty trained to (mostly) avoid those, but her early diaper use contributed to a strong loving bond with her new Mommy. As she is happy with her situation due to this relationship and her new family she's accepted being permanently in wet diapers. We consider this a positive outcome as although she's constantly in wet diapers it's through her own choice, and the bladder control could be regained should she ever change her mind.

As Benjamin's case study shows, while it can be tempting to hold until you know you're going to be checked this may be noticed, and that ability to control yourself may itself distress your Amazon. We recommend that for the first week the use of a toilet or potty should not be even mentioned or discussed with your Amazon, to demonstrate that you're comfortable with using your diapers and do not need further 'encouragement'. If (as in Evie's case) your Amazon is amenable to potty training then this can be discussed once the relationship has reached greater trust, but also assume you'll always be in diapers at least some of the time.

This will be discussed further under Rule Six, but never use words to complain about your diapers. Crying to indicate an uncomfortable diaper tends to be OK, and after the first week most Amazons will listen if you ask for a specific type of diaper (e.g. not the punishment ones) although they may not accede to the request. Complaining about the diapers, about having to wear or use them, or asking for a change almost always ends in punishment, with even the gentlest of Amazons using a pacifier to silence the complaints.

Your Amazon will check or just realize that you need a change, although it can sometimes be helpful to highlight that you're about to leak. Even then, merely point out this basic fact as it's your Amazon's responsibility to either prevent or deal with a leaking diaper, and let them make that choice.

If you are unfortunate enough to have an Amazon that defers changes (particularly messy diapers) then you will be at risk of diaper rash along with the discomfort. To help avoid this, train your Amazon to change you regularly by making the act of changing you enjoyable for her and demonstrating your gratitude for the clean diaper. While being grumpy is damaging a mild uplift in mood from before to after a change will be noticed by your Amazon and because of Rule One this will help train her.

This should be obvious from Rule Three, but never try to remove your own diaper; not only will you likely fail but this will usually lead to restraints that can even prevent you using your hands.

Other emissions[3] may be forced or inadvertent. Particularly after a liquid meal many Amazons like to burp a Little, usually holding them to their chest to do this. This is highly embarrassing, especially when the resultant burp is perhaps more liquid in nature, but again this is an issue for her to deal with, and not you. Recall Rule One and accept that she's doing this because she cares for you and feels this is good for your health and comfort, and not to humiliate you. Any other Amazon noticing will at worse think this is extremely cute, and other Littles are too used to it to try and embarrass you over it themselves.

Avoid spitting on purpose – whether eating, or any other time. If you absolutely can't avoid it, hold cloth (e.g. a bib) to your mouth and mask it as a cough or sneeze. Spitting at someone breaks Rule Two and will lead to punishment – we've even heard of one poor Little losing his tongue to prevent this.

3 Note that this pamphlet does not explore sexual activity or interactions; these vary too much on an individual basis

Although by removing your control your Amazon has accepted the burden of coping with whatever comes out of you, from either end, we've found that a small apology when being sick (especially on an Amazon) can help defuse any undeserved anger that may be caused. Combine the apology with tears and you're on track for a cuddle and forgiveness.

## *Chapter 4 : Social Interactions*

It's playtime all the time! No working for a living means you can enjoy a very early retirement and really focus on friends and hobbies.

Making friends and falling in (pretend or real) love with your Amazon is easy. Avoiding conflict with friends and family can however be a nightmare, with all the usual social challenges exacerbated by the Amazon Little divide. Going out in public is similarly fraught with dangers, some of which can not be avoided.

No matter how close to your Amazon you are, the trust you share, and the freedom you have at home to talk and make your own decisions, in public and with others you must assume the worse. They will treat you as an uncooperative baby that doesn't realize its limitations, and obeying Rule Two is paramount: Any deviation from baby behavior will result in punishment, correction or worse, sometimes even with your Amazon present and able to protect you.

*Case Study 4-Negative*: Matthew had done some great groundwork in the first month of his new relationship and impressed his Amazon with his behavior and maturity. She allowed Matty to choose his food and clothing, and they discussed challenges together in the home. Unfortunately when out shopping Matty removed his pacifier to complain about the onesie she wanted to buy him, and told her to buy a different one instead. Another Amazon overheard and contacted the protection agency, sharing a concern that Matty was being properly looked after. Following a clearly corrupt investigation Matty's Amazon was ruled incapable of caring for an infant, and herself regressed to baby status. Matthew was last seen en route to an Etiquette School.

*Case Study 4-Positive*: Eleanor unusually chose her own Amazon and they did much planning beforehand. When Ellie moved in she was able to accelerate the relationship and they fell in love almost immediately. This created a level of trust that let them discuss going out in public, with Ellie fully adopting Rule Two and demanding her pacifier everywhere she went, supported by her watchful Mommy. By acting as a quiet well-behaved baby in public Ellie won over her Amazon's friends and made a few of her own: Eleanor is now a mother herself, although her child's father still lives with his own Mommy.

Matthew's situation demonstrates how even a single encounter can spell disaster for a Little.

## Rule Six : Never Complain

Voicing a complaint, particularly in public, is not just a very obvious sign of bad behavior: Babies don't tell their parents they're unhappy, uncomfortable, dislike some food, hate the music or want to leave. They engage non-verbally, through expressions or crying. A Little that breaks Rule Two in public with a politely worded statement (e.g. “Thank you for that wonderful meal”) may cause raised eyebrows due to the maturity of the language used, but will be complimented for politeness. Complaints receive no compliments and are instead treated as a threat to the sanctity of the Little's babyhood.

Even if the Rule Two breach of a complaint doesn't cause an issue, complaints are negative in nature and will drive a negative response. This could be as simple as a change in perception but (as with Matthew) can lead to a range of stronger responses, including various punishments or corrective actions.

Complaining can be easily avoided by exploiting Rule Four, but also by understanding the situations that may cause them. Learn non-verbal cues to share discomfort or distress, or use positive interactions (e.g. reaching out to be picked up) to escape them.

Another key cause of complaints is in response to public humiliation and embarrassment.

**Rule Seven : Don't Be Embarrassed**

Using your diaper in public will happen. Right now you'll be thinking that's horrifically embarrassing but.. remember Rule Two? Babies don't get embarrassed about it, it's just part of life. Anyway, there's much worse (such as getting your used diaper changed in public). So don't let this get to you, accept that you have no personal privacy and embrace that nobody else is remotely bothered when you're half-naked being wiped down ahead of some fresh clean padding and a nice warm bottle. Relax and enjoy being pampered, and make a show of taking pleasure from it. That'll make Mommy happy too.

As you spend more time with specific individuals (Amazon or Little) you'll learn their views and expectations. Be cynical and manipulate them just as you do your own Amazon, but act constructively as you do – they can help make your life fun and engaging and give you opportunities to add meaning to your own and to their lives. Building good relationships is healthy for everybody and key to retaining your mental health.

*Chapter 5 : Punishment*

Be kind and generous, and punish your Amazon only when needed.

Punishments and correctional actions are a part of any life, but feature strongly in a relationship between an Amazon and a Little. While Amazons have the advantage in strength they are emotionally vulnerable, and this opens opportunities to punish them for transgressions.

Be cautious about this. Actions to punish an Amazon should avoid inviting retribution (so no, don't throw your food at her!) but more subtle options exist. As an example, withdrawing even a small amount of compassion or attachment can have a noticeable effect, although we do caution against completely cold-shouldering her as that can cause anger and resentment.

Punishments against you will regrettably be unavoidable, warranted or otherwise. The frequency and severity can however be greatly mitigated and much of this pamphlet works to that end, but there are some further direct ways to help.

## Rule Eight : Be In Control

Whether you call it emotional intelligence, self-awareness or another term, having that understanding of your own emotional state can help you exert self-control that avoids negative behaviors. Amazons will label any outburst, non-personal violence and other behaviors as a tantrum, and they always punish tantrums.

If you can spot the loss of control ahead of time, you can act to prevent it. While it's seldom possible to walk (or ask to be pushed/carried) away from a situation switching mental state from 'this is upsetting me' to 'I will not let this upset me' can be all that's needed and is a fantastic skill to have. Rule Four can obviously help or if someone friendly is available ask them to hold or support you.

Sometimes all you can (or need to) do is stay silent. This may not help avoid conflict entirely, but is a key contributor to the next rule.

**Rule Nine : Do Not Defend Yourself**

Whether it's a punishment spanking (justified or otherwise), assault (by an Amazon or a Little), a provocation or anything else, never defend yourself[4]. Against another Little there will always be a carer available within seconds to save you, and an active response or retaliation will merely see you punished alongside your attacker. If the assault is from an Amazon then you're highly unlikely to succeed in defending yourself anyway, and the attempt itself will be severely punished.

*Case Study 5-Negative*: Anna had settled into a sustainable relationship with her Amazon but had never truly settled. One ordinary day she had been taken to the local park to feed the ducks and had slipped and fallen on the grass by the pond. A passing Amazon man berated Annie's guardian for failing to take care of her, and suggested Anna would be better forcibly restrained in a stroller. Already embarrassed and in pain from the fall Annie spat out her pacifier and suggested (using somewhat less diplomatic terms) that the man should keep to himself and move on. Annie's carer stepped in to prevent the man reaching her but apologized to him then turned to Annie, pulled her up and carried her to a nearby park bench where a sustained and painful spanking took place. We understand that Anna's further three month punishment in thick waddle diapers is due to end shortly.

*Case Study 5-Positive*: Cameron was almost an in-betweener, much taller and stronger than most Littles. On an overnight hospital stay

4 We are frequently asked, “What if it's a matter of life and death, or forced regression”. At those times your instincts will take over anyway, so we won't waste your time offering pointless advice.

another Little got jealous of the attention Cammie was getting from the nurse (who apparently adored such a tall little being in diapers) and when she left the room ran up, pushed him down and started to strike him with a small wooden train. Although Cammie could easily have overpowered his assailant the report his Amazon later received stated admiration for how he put his hands behind his back and waited calmly until a different nurse ran over and pulled away the attacker. Cameron suffered only bruises and has since been allowed to graduate to toddler status, with the promise of daytime potty use if he can stay dry.

Don't forget the Amazonian technologies that mean even a nasty wound can be quickly healed. Momentary pain is better than a lifelong punishment!

Less obvious is that Rule Nine includes verbal defenses. If you speak angrily you'll get punished, no matter how justified you are. Amazons will often say things that are provocative without even realizing it, or may just be arrogant or ignorant. Trust in your own Amazon to know what's best for you, and to speak up in your defense if needed. And remember Rule Seven; if someone's talking about how badly your diaper smells, that's their problem not yours. You (probably) didn't choose to fill it.

## *Chapter 6 : Sustenance*

Eat, drink and be merry. It's not a cliche once you've tasted that Amazon food.

Seriously, we know some Littles that have signed up with an Amazon just to get access to the Little food you can only buy from the Amazon stores. That stuff can be addictive but that's not because of any pharmacologicals, it just tastes so good. Unfortunately the Amazons know this and ration it carefully, with the bulk of the food ranging from great (if it's what the Amazons eat) to bland to grotesque (pureed kale baby food? Yuck!)

## Rule Ten : Always eat what you're fed

Many Amazons don't believe in feeding solids to small Littles, and like to provide a liquid or pureed diet even to larger ones. This can be very unpleasant, both going in and on the way out, but an unstated facet of Rule Ten is that you're going to be made to eat it anyway. So open up, let them put it in your mouth, close, chew (if needed) and swallow. Your facial expression will share your views on the food, so let that provide the feedback and earn yourself some karma by being easy to feed.

That doesn't mean you can't refuse food; sometimes Amazons don't know when a Little is full so if you've just been fed too much and you're feeling full, that's the time to close your mouth instead of accepting the spoon/fork/spork. Even there, close it once or twice to make it clear you'd like to stop, but don't say anything and don't keep it closed after that. If you've grimaced through a pound of pureed cabbage, gravy and beetroot without complaint and only then stopped accepting it your Amazon will realize that this means you're probably full.

If they do want to keep going, let them – remember, it's their responsibility if you're sick, not yours. In the first week that may happen a couple of times, then your Amazon will know you're not bluffing and only feed you until you're full. Other Amazons (nurses, daycare attendants, etc) will show more caution as they won't know your limit and will avoid risking sickness.

*Case Study 6-Negative*: Charles was adopted by a caring pair of Amazons that started him on solid food. On his first day he resisted being fed, wanting to hold his own cutlery and show his ability to feed himself. Charlie's Amazons worried that this meant he wasn't ready for solid food and put his meal into the blender, then tried again. A second refusal led to a call to a helpful doctor, who recommended a liquid diet. Poor Charles has been fed from a bottle ever since.

*Case Study 6-Positive*: Tamina started at the other end of the scale, being fed from a bottle for her first week. A few days into her relationship Tammy had finished her bottle and reached out towards her Amazon's plate with a gentle grasping motion. She was rewarded with a small corner of Lasagna which she chewed carefully and swallowed with a big smile. When pulled from her high chair at the end of the meal Tammy reached around and gave the tightest cuddle she could in thanks, and got a smile and cuddle back. Better yet, Tamina is now on solid food for her evening meal each day.

Even when fed solids your Amazon will want you to drink a lot, and usually drink from a bottle. Rule Ten still applies; bottles suck (sorry) but they're better than getting 'treatment' because you won't drink from one.

They're not all that a lady Amazon will want you to drink from. Even though she hasn't given birth her body will respond as though you're a baby and produce some food for you.

## Rule Eleven : Go For It

Going from an adult life to being treated as a baby is tough. Being expected to breastfeed feels a step too far for many. Worse, Amazon breast milk can cause dual incontinence, and who wants that?

Well, sorry to tell you this, but you do. It'll make Rule Five easier to keep, and it'll wear off once you wean. Being reversible makes breastfeeding one of least destructive ways an Amazon can make you incontinent, so give her this option. She'll also appreciate it greatly, as her milk will need to go somewhere, and she'd rather you nurse than she pumps it herself. She'll get that physical relief, and the increased emotional attachment that any nurse gets from an infant.

There's another thing: It tastes great! You'll enjoy it too. Rule Eleven really has almost no downsides at all, once you're past that squeamish first step. That 'almost'? Never ever bite. The moment she feels teeth you're at risk of losing them. All of them. Forever. If you ever want to chew solid food, make sure you're a very gentle feeder when you're getting milk from source.

## *Chapter 7 : Day Care*

Dodge the Day Care nightmare. The only winning strategy is not to play.

Amazons love Day Care. They drop you off, then go and spend their day doing things without you. Sure, they need to go to work, or have to travel or have other things going on, but.. they're not the one trapped in daycare.

### Rule Twelve : Dodge Day Care

Do whatever you can to avoid getting put into Day Care. The best approach is to find another Amazon you can both trust that can babysit or that you can visit. They'll know you, understand you and do their best to look after you. Day Care.. won't.

It's not that the staff in Day Care facilities are evil, or malicious. They just make mistakes, get overworked, misunderstand and.. things go wrong. Permanently wrong. Hypnosis, sending you home with the wrong person, programming the robot badly.

Ah, the robots. Many Day Cares use robot assistants, either to save staff costs or because they genuinely think this is a superior choice.

## Rule Thirteen : Avoid Robots

If you thought Day Care was bad (and it is) then it's nothing compared to robot carers. They're implacable, they'll complete their programmed task whether it's right or wrong, and they make mistakes. Terrible mistakes.

You can't plead with a robot. You can't point out that it's disobeying your Amazon's strict instructions. You certainly can't wriggle free. Whether it's in a Day Care or something the mother-in-law bought, it's a threat to your safety. Help your Amazon understand your fear and horror of robots and try to avoid ever being in their care.

*Case Study 7-Negative*: Christine loved her first day at Day Care. The staff made her welcome, she met several Littles and made some new friends. Chrissie begged her Amazon to send her back, and went another eight times in the next two weeks. We never did find out what happened after that, we just know that Chrissie came home from that final visit unable to walk and with a terrified glaze on her eyes. After an in-depth review we canceled our rescue attempt as Christine now genuinely needs the care she's receiving from her Amazon.

*Case Study 7-Positive*: Edward was curious about Day Care and didn't fight being sent. He did realize straight away that this was a dangerous place and focused on obeying all instructions but otherwise being quiet and fairly withdrawn. In Eddy's second week the center was short of staff and instead of giving him a needed change a robot assistant was sent over to help him. As it started to strip him down Eddy heard the robot declare, “Processing 6 month old girl” and realized the robot was still set for its previous patient, a smaller female Little. Rather than struggle, fight and get both hurt and punished Eddy resolved himself to the inevitable, which included removal of all his hair and a well fitting pink diaper with accompanying dress. On her return to the Day Care

Eddy's Amazon couldn't decide whether to comfort him or berate the Day Care, but did vow never to send him there again. Edward now has a regular baby sitter that properly addresses his needs.

In this entire publication you are encouraged and provided with tools to avoid punishment. Rule Twelve is the exception: It's worth getting punished if it keeps you out of Day Care.

## *Chapter 8 : Trust and Intimacy*

Build that bond and benefit from it.

By now you should have a strong bond with your Amazon. You'll know her limits, what she'll tolerate, what you can get away with. Use this information, exploit it and strengthen that relationship. You may be together for years to come, so make them fun and full of love.

### Rule Fourteen : Have Fun

Find shared interests, or ways to pursue your own hobbies. If you both like the countryside, get out there. If you both enjoy knitting, ask for some wool. You're an intelligent creative being, you need that stimulation and it'll make you happier, so help your Amazon understand this and provide it to you.

*Case Study 8-Negative*: Terence had never forgiven his Amazon for adopting him, and refused to try and like her. The Amazon loved Terry despite this, but couldn't work out how to keep him happy and he gave her no help in this. After months of failing to find things he could enjoy she conceded and went with her mother's suggestion: Terence was regressed to a mental age of 8 months, although he does seem happier now

*Case Study 8-Positive*: Victoria had also never forgiven her Amazon but recognized the need for an amicable relationship. Vicky worked hard on being well behaved and built enough trust to be allowed to pick up her hobbies. Not only was Vicky happier, this made her Amazon happier too, and also gave Vicky the chance to meet other Littles and contact us. Victoria escaped through our network two months ago and helped review this publication.

It's not a betrayal to have fun with your Amazon. You need and deserve some fun in your life, so get it where you can.

## *Chapter 9 : Ending Your Relationship*

Escape. Flee, into the night, never to return.

All good things come to an end. But how will your story finish?

### Rule Fifteen : Choose

This pamphlet collates the guidance we've been giving to Littles for many years now and just owning a copy of it will get you sent to Etiquette School. Hope you can trust the person from whom you received it, and ask them to put you in touch with us. We'll do our best to get you free!

But we've found that those that obey the rules, build the relationships and get themselves to a position from which escape is possible generally don't want to. They find they like their new life and are happy for it to continue.

If that's you, don't be ashamed. You're in a good place, go and be happy.

www.ingramcontent.com/pod-product-compliance
Lightning Source LLC
LaVergne TN
LVHW041132150826
845673LV00007B/2295
*9781999319922*